Library of Congress catalog card number: 2003103536
Printed in the U.S.A.
Book design by Joe Merkel

1  2  3  4  5  6  7  8  9  10
❖
First Edition

www.harperchildrens.com
www.spykids.com

# Meet the Spy Kids

ADAPTED BY KATE EGAN

BASED ON THE SCREENPLAY BY

ROBERT RODRIGUEZ

HarperFestival®

*A Division of* HarperCollins*Publishers*

We are Carmen and Juni Cortez,

two of the best kid spies in the world!

We are good at keeping secrets.

We are also good at telling stories.

This is the story of our lives as spies so far.

A long time ago,

we were just a couple of normal kids.

Or so we *thought*.

Our parents were famous spies.

But that was a big secret—

especially to us.

Then our parents disappeared!

And that is how we became spy kids.

Suddenly we had our first spy mission.

We had to save our parents!

Mom and Dad had been captured
by a bad guy named Floop.
Floop wanted something called
the Third Brain.

Floop was building an army of robot kids.
The Third Brain would make them smart.
Then Floop and the robots could take
over the world.

There was one big problem.

Our parents didn't have the Third Brain.

Floop would be mad when he found

out they couldn't help him.

He would turn Mom and Dad into

strange creatures called Fooglies . . .

. . . unless we found them first.

We were ready to go undercover!

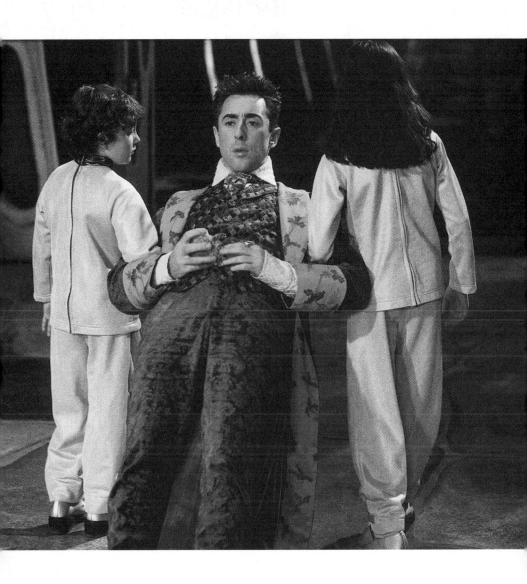

We flew our spy plane to Floop's castle.

(He was not a king, but he lived like one.)

We had to swim past sleeping sharks!

We had to slip past Thumb-Thumb guards!

At last, we found our way in.

The robots were ready to attack—
even the robots that looked like us!

Luckily, we had some spy gadgets
to help us.

We found our parents just in time.

Then we faced the robots together.

There were four spies in
our family now.

Rescuing our parents was just
the first of our dangerous missions.
The next one took us to a
mysterious island.
A strange inventor lived there.
What was he up to?

Our gadgets couldn't help us.

They wouldn't work on this island.

But good spies are smart.

We figured the inventor was hiding

something big.

He was hiding something called
the Transmooker!
It could shut down every
computer in the world.

Someone had to get it back.

It was a job for spy kids!

So, we took off in a magnetic hovercraft.

We hid out in an underwater cave.

We battled some skeleton pirates.

We finally got to the Transmooker.

Then we made a big mistake.

We turned it on!

For a minute, the whole world stopped.

Luckily, we had one gadget

that still worked.

It was just a rubber band,

but it did the trick.

We saved the day again.

We saved the world again.

Our latest mission was our riskiest yet.
It took us into another world—
inside a computer!

It began when Carmen hacked into a virtual reality game.

She was supposed to shut it down.

Instead, she got stuck inside of it!

OSS called Juni to the rescue!

He put on his 3-D glasses.

With help from some new friends,

he fought through four levels of the game.

We spy kids shut it down together.

But that was not the end.

Some robots had escaped from the computer!

We had to find them in real life—before they destroyed our city.

People in the real world couldn't
see the robots.

But our 3-D glasses helped us find them.

Our family helped us find them, too!

Once again, the world was safe—

thanks to the Cortezes!

We love being spy kids!

We are always busy.

We are never bored.

And we never know what

will happen next!